CIRCULATION
1,000,000

BIG

AND P
triking
At the
rus Re
reapi
of y
e Ty
ger
an
osa

To all who are searching
and thinking outside the box.

First American Edition 2019
Kane Miller, A Division of EDC Publishing

Text and illustration copyright © 2019 by Henning Löhlein
Design copyright © 2019 by The Templar Company Limited

First published in the UK in 2019 by Templar Publishing,
part of the Bonnier Publishing Group.

For more information contact:
Kane Miller, A Division of EDC Publishing
PO Box 470663
Tulsa, OK 74147-0663
www.kanemiller.com
www.edcpub.com
www.usbornebooksandmore.com

Library of Congress Control Number: 2018958203

Printed in China
1 3 5 7 9 10 8 6 4 2

ISBN 978-1-61067-864-3

Henning Löhlein

LUDWIG THE TIME DOG

Kane Miller
A DIVISION OF EDC PUBLISHING

Ludwig and his friends lived
in a world of books.
One day they were playing
in their favorite story,
when the postman arrived.

He had a parcel for Ludwig, and it was a very strange shape.

49

It was an egg! In fact, it was the biggest egg Ludwig had ever seen.

There was also a note from Ludwig's friend Peter the Penguin:

Dear Ludwig,
I found this on my travels, but I have run out of time to take it back to its mommy. Can you, old friend? It will be an adventure for you!

From Peter the Penguin x

Ludwig was very excited. He wanted to set off on his adventure straightaway.

Travel the World

But where was he going,
and who *was* the egg's mommy?

Peter hadn't said where the egg was from—
though Ludwig's friends had lots of ideas.

I WONDER HOW THIS WORKS . . .

Ludwig looked at some books about animals to find out which ones lay eggs.

He learned that elephants don't . . .

. . . but that most lizards do. It was too big to be a lizard egg, though . . .

Eidechsen II.

Ludwig and his friend Mac had once explored a book about digging up the past. Ludwig didn't think they'd find the egg's mommy in there though—it had just been full of old bones.

But then he remembered a useful book he'd never looked at before.

It was very deep and so old it was full of holes made by hungry bookworms. Ludwig had always been scared of getting lost in there.

He climbed up, and leapt through a hole in the cover.

Then he started to fall.

VICTORIAN SCIENCE

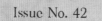

Soon, Ludwig landed in the past.
People wore funny clothes, so he knew
it must be a long time ago.
He asked a scientist if the egg's mommy
lived there, but the scientist said no.

IT'S MUCH
OLDER THAN THIS!
LEAVE IT WITH ME.
I WILL CONDUCT
SOME EXPERIMENTS.

The lady there looked carefully
at the egg and told Ludwig he had
to go farther back in time.
Ludwig hadn't thought that was
possible, but he held the egg tightly,
closed his eyes, and jumped.

...and landed in a magnificent palace. He met someone there who seemed very interested in the egg.

WOW! I WONDER IF THE EGG'S MOMMY LIVES HERE.

THAT EGG WILL MAKE A WONDERFUL OMELET FOR THE EMPEROR!

Ludwig decided he didn't want to hang around. History was a tough place to be an egg!

Then he and the egg tumbled through the longest, deepest tunnel they had been through yet.

Just when Ludwig thought
he'd keep falling forever . . .

But it wasn't!
Coming through the trees were
the most enormous, terrifying
creatures Ludwig had ever seen.
He'd only ever read about them
in books before—they were
dinosaurs!

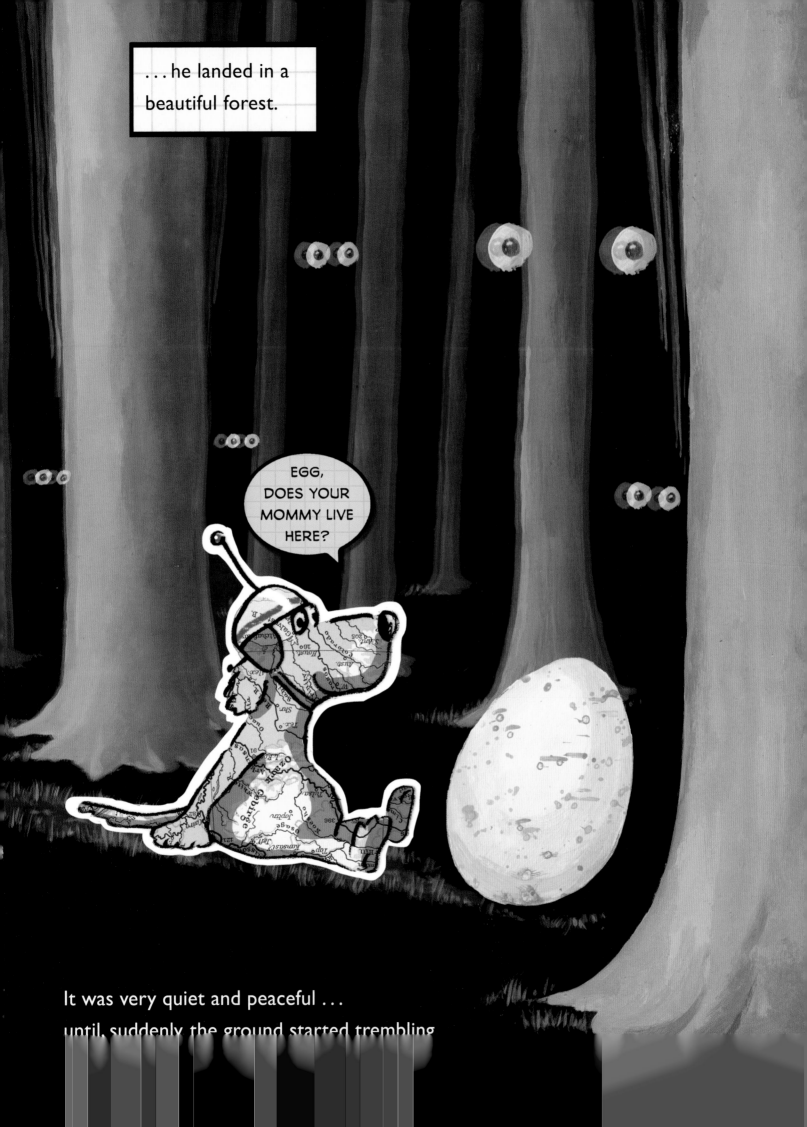

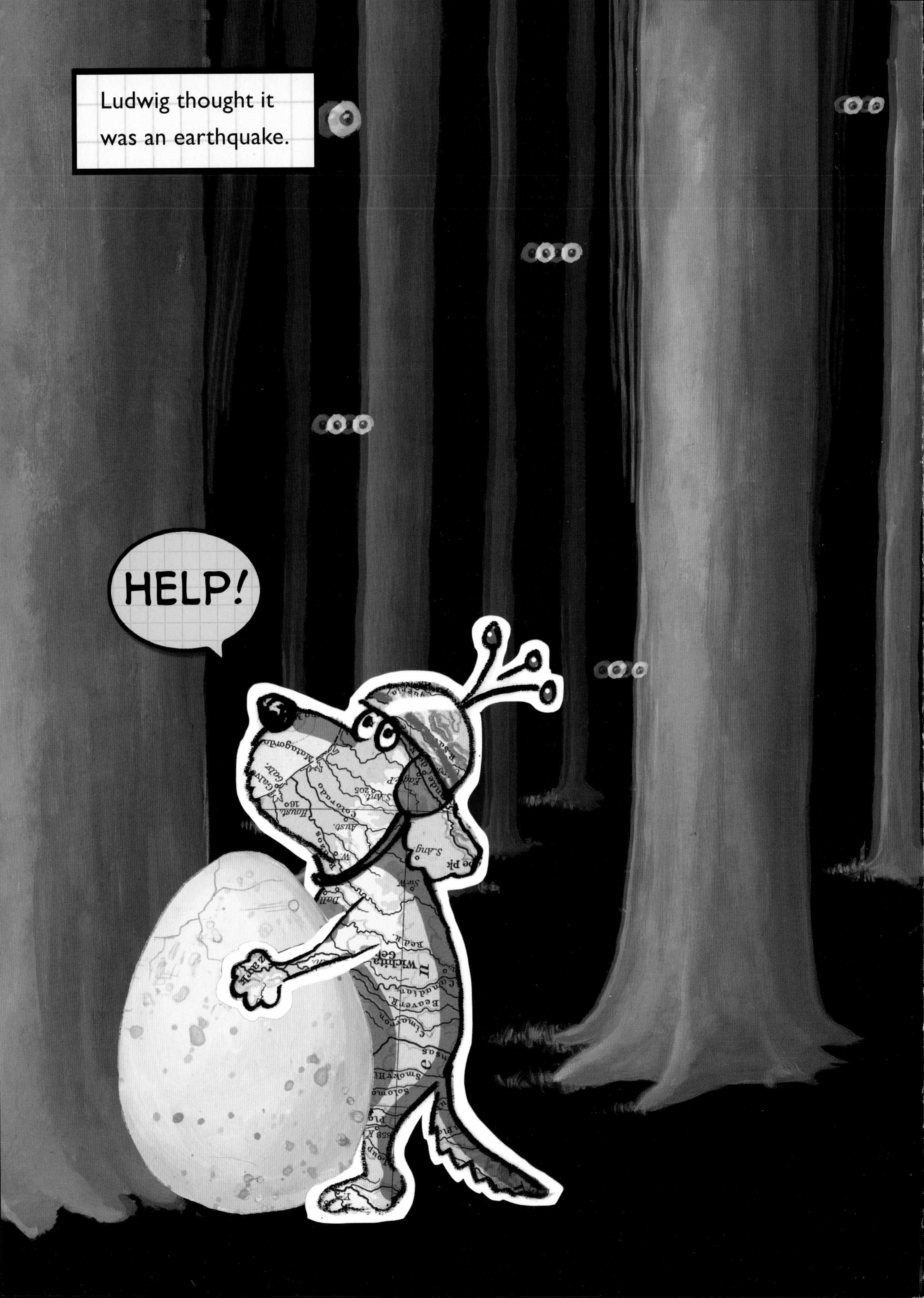
Ludwig thought it was an earthquake.
HELP!

Ludwig wanted to run away,
but he had to look after the egg.

It had started to crack—the baby
inside was ready to hatch!

Ludwig held the egg tightly.
The dinosaurs came closer,
and he trembled with fear.

Then the egg broke open!

I HAVE TO LOOK AFTER THE BABY IN THIS EGG.

Inside was a baby dinosaur!

And its mommy was right there.

IT WAS A DINOSAUR EGG!

MOMMY!

The mommy dinosaur was very pleased to have her baby back.

And Ludwig asked her if she could help him get home.

I GOT HERE THROUGH HOLES THE BOOKWORMS MADE IN THE PAGES, BUT I CAN'T GET BACK UP!

The dinosaur lifted Ludwig up to the nearest hole,
but he still couldn't reach it.

Then, he saw something he recognized.

It was Enzo's watch!
Ludwig held on tight.

Soon he was back with his friends. As soon as he could,
he wrote to Peter the Penguin about his adventures.